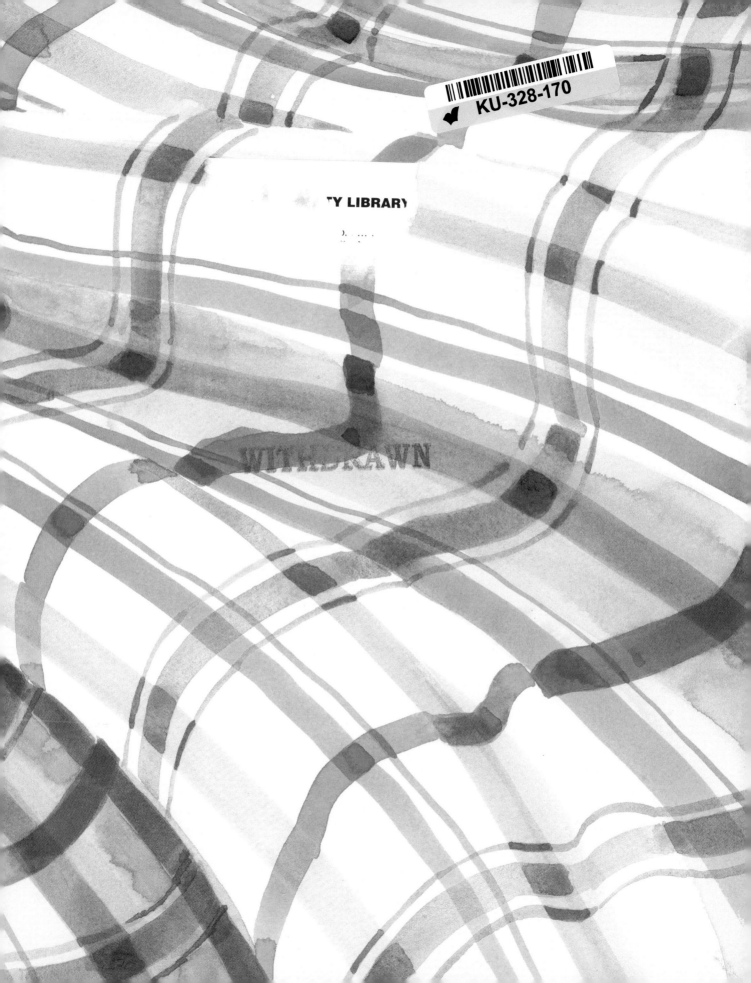

A Galway Fairytale

For my lovely dad, Alfie Sweeney.

First published 2021 by The O'Brien Press Ltd,

12 Terenure Road East, Rathgar, Dublin 6, D06 HD27, Ireland.

Tel: +353 I 4923333; Fax: +353 I 4922777

E-mail: books@obrien.ie

Website: www.obrien.ie

The O'Brien Press is a member of Publishing Ireland.

ISBN: 978-1-78849-224-9

7 6 5 4 3 2 I

24 23 22 21

Printed and bound in Poland by Białostockie Zakłady Graficzne S.A.

The paper in this book is produced using pulp from managed forests.

**Caitriona Sweeney is a writer and illustration artist from Dublin. This is
her fourth book as an illustrator, but the first she has written as well as
illustrated. She is an admirer of nice woolly jumpers, so enjoyed painting
several of them into this book.**

A Galway Fairytale receives financial assistance from the Arts Council

Published in:

DUBLIN
UNESCO
City of Literature

A Galway
Fairytale

Caitriona Sweeney

THE O'BRIEN PRESS
DUBLIN

Once upon a time, a brother and sister called
Seán and Gráinne lived beside the sea in
Galway with their mam and dad.

'It's Mam's birthday today,'
said Gráinne. 'May we go to
town to buy her a present?'
Dad thought this
was a great idea.
'You could buy her
a Claddagh ring,'
he said.

'Hurry. Don't be long and don't stop to buy sweets. We'll
have some at the birthday party when you get back.'

Seán and Gráinne loved an adventure! They packed a
rucksack with some brown soda bread and jam in case they
got hungry.

When they got to Spanish Arch they got a fright to see a man with a big sword.

'If you give me
some of that
nice bread I'll
let you pass,'
the man said.
Seán and Gráinne
didn't mind sharing so they
broke him off a piece, dropping
crumbs as they did so, and they
went on their way.

9

By the Salmon Weir Bridge they stopped for a moment beside a woman in a cloak who was watching the salmon leaping upstream.

11

'Will we throw some of that bread to the fish from the bridge?' the woman suggested. Seán and Gráinne thought this was a great idea – they loved to see the salmon leaping too!

'We'd better hurry on,' said Gráinne.

'Yes, we don't want to be late for Mam's birthday,' replied Seán. 'Let's go!'

On they walked towards Eyre Square, where they looked over at the boat sculpture.

Looking closer they were surprised to see a man who seemed to be fishing.

The man waved to them. 'Can I have some of your bread to give to the birds?' he shouted.

Their bread was almost gone, but they shared some with him and helped him throw crumbs to the birds.

Finally Seán and Gráinne arrived at the market.

There was lots to see and so
many different things for sale.

The air smelled of cakes and
buns and lovely things to eat.

18

After looking at all the different stalls and listening to the music, they went to the jewellery stall and bought the perfect ring for Mam.

Delighted that they had the Claddagh ring for Mam, the children turned for home. They hadn't gone far when they realised they were lost.

'I don't remember this street,' said Gráinne looking around. They were standing outside a sweet shop so full of mouth-watering treats that it almost looked like it was made of sweets and chocolate and gingerbread!

The door opened, 'Come in, come in,' said a voice.
'Try some of my delicious sweets.'

She shut the door behind them and locked it.

'Ha! I have you now and I want that Claddagh ring! Give it to me!'

'NO!' shouted Seán and Gráinne, 'it's for our mam.
You can't have it!'

The fisherman was passing the shop and heard all the noise. 'Who is shouting in the witch's shop?' he wondered. 'It's those nice children who shared their bread with me!'

He called his friend, the woman with the cloak.
'Those nice children who shared their bread are trapped
in the witch's shop! Come help me rescue them!'

She shouted to the man with the sword.
'Those nice children who shared their bread
are trapped in the witch's shop! Come help us rescue them!'

The man with the sword, the woman with
the cloak and the fisherman all banged on
the door of the sweet shop until they got in
and rescued the children.

When Seán and Gráinne got outside, with Mam's ring safe in Gráinne's bag, they thanked their new friends for rescuing them.

'We'd better hurry home with Mam's ring now,' said Gráinne. 'We don't want to miss her party!'

'But how will we find our way home?' asked Seán.

Their three new friends pointed to
the trail of breadcrumbs. 'Follow
this and you'll get home safely.'

Seán and Gráinne thanked their friends and, sure enough, the crumbs led them all the way home.

Mam and Dad were delighted to see them. Mam proudly wore her new Claddagh ring while Dad buttered more soda bread for everyone in the warm kitchen.

The Claddagh ring represents love (heart), friendship (hands) and loyalty (crown). It's named after the Claddagh area of Galway where it was first created in the 17th Century.

Built in 1584 to protect ships from looting, Galway's Spanish Arch commemorates Ireland's trading links with Spain. Spanish ships often docked here, carrying wine, silks and spices from lands far away.